Little Kunoichi
The Ninja Girl

WITHDRAWN

Written and Illustrated
by SANAE ISHIDA

little bigfoot
an imprint of sasquatch books
seattle, wa

On a super secret island . . .

there is a super,
super secret village.

Hidden in the valley amid bamboo forests, Treehouse Village is home to many ninja families.

This is **Little Kunoichi** (*koo·no·ee·chee*). She is a ninja-girl-in-training who lives with her father, mother, and baby brother. Oh, and her pet bunny.

THE FAMILY

DAD   MOM   BRO   PET

Little Kunoichi goes to
a very special school.

SHOULD HAVE WORN THE BLACK ONE...

HELP!

The lessons are challenging . . .

NAME LITTLE KUNOICHI

0/15

☐ Climbing

☐ Hiding

☐ Star-throwing

☐ Nunchucks

Please stay after school

Sometimes she sneaks
off to her hideaway in
the bamboo forest.

What to do, what to do?
School is so hard.

Suddenly . . .

What is this?
WHO is this?

YAH!

It's Chibi Samurai. He is from a nearby village and goes to a special school too.

CHIBI SAMURAI

He is very, very little. And perhaps not the best samurai-in-training.

Little Kunoichi watches
Chibi Samurai practice.

PHYSICAL FITNESS

1...2...UGH!

STRATEGY

"GO" GAME

MINDFULNESS

SNORE!

And practice
and practice
and practice . . .

Little Kunoichi starts to practice . . .

and practice and practice too.

An unexpected encounter happens one day.

"Hi," says Chibi Samurai.

"Hi," says Little Kunoichi.

"I like your *shugyo* style," he says.

"Shugyo?"

"It means training like crazy.
Want to shugyo together?"

"Yes!"

Little Kunoichi and Chibi Samurai are excited. After weeks of practicing together, they feel ready to showcase their skills.

They plan and plan to come up with something spectacular to wow the crowd.

Are there any unicorns on the island?

And aren't they usually white?

Or could we make something out of wood?

Where are Little Kunoichi and Chibi Samurai?
They are getting ready. What a crowd!

Ta-da! They pull it off! Sword-wielding and star-throwing in a flying boat! (Sort of. It's really hanging from a beam.)

"Oops! We're sorry Dragon-san! We missed the target.
At least we added extra pizzazz to the festival!"

OUCH!

Shugyo is the way
The goal: better, not perfect
Practice and have fun

CHIBI SAMURAI
good!

LITTLE KUNOICHI
MUCH IMPROVED!

Did you find Little Kunoichi and Chibi Samurai in the festival crowd? See the image to the right for their hiding spots.

Did you know?

Kunoichi actually means "female ninja" in Japanese. If you take the Kanji character for "woman," which looks like this: 女 and pull it apart, it creates the word *kunoichi*. Like this:

女 = く ノ 一 = 🥷

Shugyo is a concept important to eastern philosophy. It is about training like crazy to gain mastery. All samurais and ninjas are expected to *shugyo*.

Chibi means "small" or "short." Samurais were noble warriors in olden Japan. They were also known as *bushi*. Samurais were not only trained in weaponry, but they were also highly educated. Samurai women were called *onna-bugeisha*.

Taiko drums are huge and frequently part of festivals. Two people (each on one side) can drum at the same time.

Sumo wrestling is an ancient Japanese sport and is still hugely popular in Japan today. The average sumo wrestler weighs over 400 pounds!

Women and men used to wear kimonos as daily wear. Nowadays, they are worn mainly for special occasions, like weddings and festivals.

Ninjas were trained in ancient martial arts, acrobatics, stealth, and cunning. Japanese royal families hired them to carry out dangerous missions. There are no known active ninjas. Today, the word is used for someone who is excellent at a particular skill.

Go is a board game originally from China that is popular in Japan. It requires strategy and patience.

Who is that baby in a peach? And that boy in a bowl in the festival crowd? They are characters from traditional folk tales. The peach boy is from the story *Momotaro*, and the boy in the bowl, "Little One Inch," is from the tale *Issun Boshi*.

Little Kunoichi and Chibi Samurai call the dragon *Dragon-san*. In Japan, adding "-san" to the end of a name is a sign of respect.

For my ninja tribe
K + M

Manufactured in China by C&C Offset Printing Co. Ltd. Shenzhen, Guangdong Province, in November 2014

Published by Little Bigfoot, an imprint of Sasquatch Books

20 19 18 17 16 15   9 8 7 6 5 4 3 2 1

Editor: Tegan Tigani
Project editor: Nancy W. Cortelyou
Illustrations: Sanae Ishida
Design: Joyce Hwang

Library of Congress Cataloging-in-Publication Data is available.

ISBN: 978-1-57061-954-0

Sasquatch Books
1904 Third Avenue, Suite 710
Seattle, WA 98101
(206) 467-4300
www.sasquatchbooks.com
custserv@sasquatchbooks.com